D0621120

WITHDRAWN
University

University

Philip Booth's new collection confronts—
and survives—emptiness, sovereign of the
realm before sleep. His forty-three poems
and their interspersed sequence of "Night
Notes" form a kind of whole, in which the
units are compelled into larger shape by a
counternarrative that performs a choral as
well as a thematic function. The subject is
that of growing older; here the poet as a man
stops to consider and survey the path of his
accumulated days because meditation is the
only way he can arrest the perpetual and
irreversible process of which he writes. He
fashions a song of convergence between
himself, family, town, and nature as a method
of ordering what his mind conjures through-
out his night notes and their daytime reflec-
tions. The poetry moves unflinchingly
through the ills and losses of mid-life, admits
mourning, invokes memory to regain
balance, and resiliently speaks for coming to
terms with the coming of age.

Whether he is remembering his parents or
Hannah Arendt or Robert Lowell, or being
amused by, and musing on, the wonder of
his grandson; whether he is talking about
finding words to craft, or walking on ances-
tral ground toward the sea at night, or
working wood, the tick of the clock is always
audible, the sense of a shadow present and of
something being lost. And yet, there is also a
constant coming back to self against the pull
of doubt in the notes, until the center of grav-
ity is reached, the still point of the circle,
which is the knowledge of where one is in
one's own life. As they build toward new per-
spectives, and face the raw beauty of "how
today feels," these poems reach out to vali-
date our lives in pointing both to the dark
night of the soul and to the survival that such
night makes possible.

Also by Philip Booth

PS
3552
.O647
B4

BEFORE SLEEP

POEMS BY
PHILIP BOOTH

PACIFIC UNIVERSITY LIBRARY
FOREST GROVE OREGON

THE VIKING PRESS
NEW YORK

Copyright © Philip Booth, 1976, 1977, 1978, 1979, 1980
All rights reserved
First published in 1980 by The Viking Press
625 Madison Avenue, New York, N.Y. 10022
Published simultaneously in Canada by
Penguin Books Canada Limited

LIBRARY OF CONGRESS CATALOGING IN PUBLICATION DATA
Booth, Philip E
Before sleep.
I. Title.
PS3552.O647B4   811'.54   80-14995
ISBN 0-670-15529-2

Printed in the United States of America
Set in CRT Garamond

Thanks to the editors of the following journals for permission to reprint these poems:

"Dayrise," "Eaton's Boatyard," "Old Man," "Mary's, After Dinner," "Still Life," and "Wonder," *American Poetry Review;* "Lichens" and "Tools," *Antaeus;* "Building Her," "Fog," and "Syntax," *The Atlantic Monthly;* "The Young," *Choomia;* "Middling," *Crazyhorse;* "Calendar," "Out of the Ordinary," and "Rates," *Field;* "This Day after Yesterday," *The Georgia Review;* "A Slow Breaker," "Here," "The Valley Road," *The Hudson Review;* "Continuum," "Flinching," and "Generation," *The Missouri Review;* "Of Whales and Men: 1864" and "Thinking About Hannah Arendt," *The Nation;* "Liv," *New Letters;* "Bicentennium" and "Dragging," *The New Republic;* "Gathering Greens," "Ossipee: November," and "Thoreau Near Home," *The New Yorker;* "Sorting It Out," *Ploughshares;* "Before Sleep," "Not to Tell Lies," and "Words for the Room," *Poetry Northwest;* "A Vespertide" and "Matter," *Quest;* and "Falling Apart," *Shenandoah.*

*To the memory of
my mother*

*after all
these years*

Poems/*Night Notes*

BEFORE SLEEP

Not to Tell Lies

He has come to a certain age.
To a tall house older than he is.
Older, by far, than he ever will be.
He has moved his things upstairs, to a room
which corners late sun. It warms a schooner model,
his daughter's portrait, the rock his doctor brought him
back from Amchitka. When he looks at the rock he thinks Melville;
when he touches the lichen he dreams Thoreau. Their testaments
shelve the inboard edge of the oak-legged table he writes on.
He has nailed an ancestor's photograph high over his head.
He has moored his bed perpendicular to the North wall;
whenever he rests his head is compassed barely west
of Polaris. He believes in powers: gravity, true
North, magnetic North, love. In how his wife
loved the year of their firstborn. When-
ever he wakes he sees the clean page in
his portable. He has sorted life out;
he feels moved to say all of it,
most of it all. He tries
to come close, he keeps
coming close: he has
gathered himself
in order not
to tell
lies.

Aside from the life
I live inside it,
this room is nothing.
Nothing invades it.
I try to figure: I
am more vital than it;
that is my virtue: not
in my own life to live
as if nothing
were more important.

Words for the Room

Today's a long season after Thanksgiving.
I got up early, let out the dogs, and ate.
I've got almost four almost-right poems,

and one quick typewriter set before me,
plus a silvery Piels Real Draft, already
half empty at my left hand. I sit

on the right hand of Saint Jarrell, despairing,
trying to mind an old heart that is, in spite
of itself, almost full. I love my children,

I'm stunned by my grandson, renewed by my wife.
I almost have poems. And, to complete them,
hundreds of words, a whole dark roomful to choose from.

Words for the room: a new ceiling, a door.
That's all, they're all, between me and the world;
nothing but choice, nothing save will:

infinitives, relative objects. I can feel,
I can name, what I have to decide: I mean
if I mean to revise my whole life.

In this gray depression
I try to sleep off, or
wake from, nothing connects.
Nothing gets to me. In that
there is nothing to say,
I have to begin with nothing.
In that there is nothing
to feel, there's nothing
I'd better question. I find
myself far into mid-life
willing at last to begin.

Falling Apart

The windows stay.
The clapboards go wavy.
The high branches look
to belong to the elm.

It's inside things
don't arrive right: how
far from my good eye
this left fist is; or
this swelled thumb. How long
my neck has refused to
hold up its head. Parts
of me disincline; I lean
in a lot of directions,
all without compass.

There isn't fog, but
it's gray all day: gray
in the elms' old elbows,
gray in my bowels. Cracks
in the clapboard want paint.
My hand thinks my head
needs more room on the sill.
There are holes where some-
body took out the nails.

Only the windows stay.

Flinching

Crossing from where he has been
to where he even less wants to go,

hollow of sleep, faced by the moon,
he feels animals in him eat at their reins.

Marooned between lines of opposing traffic,
he tries to get off the island ledge:

he prays to Kochab, and wakes without sun,
the morning opera already howling.

Distrusting the natives two valleys west,
he steals along clamflats; waves

breed waves twice as high as his head:
wherever he moves is over the edge.

Out of the Ordinary

Halfway south, in one
of hundreds of would-be cities
ending in -*ville*,
                    he looked at dusk
out his motel window: a blackwoman
gardened the narrow strip between
the cementblock walls
                    where he'd sleep
and where her own clapboards
faded toward white. A dog's lope beyond,
across the sideroad,
                    a slow-pitch game
was beginning under the long-stemmed lights.
Over their flowering, nighthawks stunted;
the thinnest possible moon
                    was just making up.
Out of the ordinary, too tired to rest,
he stood and looked: he looked and looked
for the joy of it.

Noam was in intensive care when he came to.
The truck hit the taxi, the taxi jumped the curb,
sideswiped him and felled his wife, then twisted
back at him.

              Heigh-ho, the dairy-o,
she'd just gone out to buy milk . . .

Noam saw the replay before the nurse came on:
Don't worry, *she said,* you're going
to be all right. Nothing
is going to happen.
I know, *Noam said,* it already has.

Matter

No matter what you do
or don't, or imagine,

the tree you live by
is bound to come down.

Maybe not in your lifetime.
Without doubt in its own.

Of Whales and Men: 1864

The possible
world:
      a man
named Svend Foyn

invented
the end:
      we began
to explode
inside:
      what struck us
stuck:
      we died,
slowly,
of the barb

charged
to tow us:
      it came
in time
to be general

practice.

A Slow Breaker

Washing on granite
before it turns
on itself, away

from every horizon
it fetched from,
this clear green wash,

the flashing, cold,
specific gravity of it,
calls the eye down

to what we thought to
look into, to all we
cannot see through.

Recall

Father,
        Without you, I drift off at work
with a dream you must have slept with
for years:
        that spanking-new '34 Chevy
parked at the top of the steep cement ramp
in the brick garage where you always bought cars
in the town I could never grow up in.

I went with you the day they delivered:
the cream wheels, the plush smell, the braided cord for
a laprobe—a car I've had stored so long
I forgot it.
        I barely wake now,
cold Aprils after your dying, to this green car
mother paid for, this dream I've slept on
for hundreds of seasons, this face in the rear-view mirror
that looks more like yours
than my own;
        I own to it now:
the way I have to reclaim what I've left,
the way I need to get myself back.

His nurse, at bedside, said What is it?
Nothing, *Noam said,* it's nothing.

He heard her keep saying I want to know.
No, *he said,* nobody wants to.

I tell you I do. I want
to know. Where does it hurt?

It doesn't, it's
nothing, nothing at all.

You're trying to cry, it's got
to be hurting.

I tell you it's nothing,
nothing is all.

Bicentennium

To a lifetime dying has touched
nothing holds
               like trying
to recover:
                front wheel drive,
studded wide-ovals, chrome headers,
steel skis:
           all that
and the girl
who goes with them:
                   they glare
at the world
             from their own
late sun.

A Vespertide

The sun, as a matter of course.
The house keeps mixing its shadows,
dark shadows and light,
into the tea, minted and iced,
a child has left on the patio table.
Beside the rowed iris
that ease the steps, the steps
the sun has already taken, white steel chairs
flex their white spring backs
like the big white cat who appears
to be part of the furniture.
There are flags planted between
the flagstones, as if a child
had invented a nation, of which
the house were writing a history
by how its shadows are, in turn,
informed by the shadows of every iris,
which deeply cool as the cat's eyes widen,
noticing what the child has forgotten
now that the sun, just in time,
has gone in.

Fog

Winded, drifting to rest,
                        I'm rowing
between islands, between pewter water
and a gauze I'm unwinding that winds back
behind me in my flat wake.
                              At the tip
of each oar small vortices whorl
at each stroke's end.
                       If I looked down through
I could see Stephen who swam for his friend
on his eighth birthday. Or Mr. Ames,
swept overboard at daybreak, racing
big seas off Greenland. Or his boys
who went after him.
                       They were my heroes
the June I was nine. It's different now:
with no horizon, with the end
of the century coming up,
                        I'm rowing
where measure is lost, I'm barely moving,
in a circle of translucence that moves with me
without compass.
                      I can't see out or up into;
I sit facing backwards,
                       pulling myself slowly
toward the life I'm still trying to get at.

Nothing is sure.
Nothing in me
approaches nothing
constantly; though
I approach nothing
at a constant rate,
the process, as
we close, seems
to accelerate.

Rates

A caterpillar, long
beyond summer, crossing
the blacktop
east of Machias

     Copernicus   Leonardo   Luther

a fingerling headed
downstream, in
an eddy

     Galileo   Shakespeare   Newton

pinwheeling out in
M-101, a white dwarf dead
before history was born

     Bach   Voltaire   Diderot   Hume

the black mark spun
through the meter down cellar,
a bulb left on in the attic
all winter

     Kant   Mozart   Blake

forsythia, barely
unfolded, out on
the outskirts
of Gander

     Darwin   Marx   Van Gogh

a tern, its beak
quick with herring,
flying up through current to
sun

       Freud   Picasso   Einstein

a far gun: while
smoke announces
something has started, air
withholding
its tall report.

Generation

A bald fifty-some,
                        shaving in
his dead father's
nickel-plated
                        extensible mirror
(patented 1902),
the father, stripped
                        to bathe, notes
his bare grandson
studying again, from
                        four-year-old
eye-level, the old
primary stem,
                        hanging out
from the apple-
pouch where he
                        remembers his father's,
presiding over
a wad of wirehair.
                        He shaves considering
all the trouble.

What's the story?

The story's this,
nothing at all
like we thought.

Middling

The first new pains
in one's body:
                    how
bone joints freeze, and
the moon tides flood
and ebb bloody.
                    Nothing
can stop them:
                    children
needing to leave,
                        parents
having to die.
                    Middling,
torn between orchards
and gravestones, we
watch the March yard
from your bed. The clock's
tick impinges:
                    How long
was it this time? Did
he say it was going to
be all right?
                    Then, within
forecast, a new wave of
bleeding . . .
                    I feel
like the bottom
just dropped out.

We used to say Nothing's
too good for our kids.

Now we don't know what to say.

*Nothing seems to be good enough
for them. If everything isn't
just right, nothing will do.*

The Young

They keep doing it.

                      Missing

the curve.

                Three, already,

in just this one year.

                     The same

stretch, three different lives.

A telephone pole, a tree,
a stonewall.

                The headlights hit

before the car rolls.

                    They keep

doing it.

                Too much or too little,

in wrong combinations, too late.
Or too early.

                  They keep missing

the curve.

             The siren.

                    And in

a dark house the darkness through
hundreds of nights after the phone
begins its blind ring.

Dragging

A whole week. Out of
the north all day.

A dry cold. The wind
clean as split oak.

Dark islands, dark as
the march of whitecaps.

Under hills hard on
the shoreline: churches,

settlements, planted
like bones. Out here,

the boat on good marks,
we let the wire out:

the drag plunges and
tugs. First light to

first dark, we tow, dump,
set, tow. Numb to what

cuts our hands, we set,
tow, dump, mend; tow until

dark closes down. We clean
the catch heading in

through dark to the thin
walls of our lives, grown

numb to the wind, numb
to the dark, to all we've

dragged for and taken,
shells returned to

that other dark that
weighs the whole bottom.

Durward: setting his trawl
for haddock, and handlining cod
a halfmile east of Seal Island,

twelve miles offshore in fog.
Then his new engine went out.
A Rockland dragger spotted him,

two days later, drifting drunk
off Mount Desert Rock. He was
down to his last sixpack.

After they towed him back in,
Ordway kept asking him what
—those two days—he'd been thinking.

Nothin. I thought about nothin.
That was all there was to it.
Ord said, Y'must've thought something.

Nope, I thought about nothin.
You know what I thought,
I thought fuckit.

Here

There
is which way the wind blows
and how:
        with what strength
and fetch,
        but the choice is
in us
       we think whether
             to search
out into it,
       and, if we do, what
course to set:

         to beat into it,
the familiar
       semblance of achievement,
feeling
     sure
        resistance
to all
     we hope to make good;

or simply reaching
         across it,
the fastest possible passage;

that, or
      easing off all
            the way,
even
    with luck
        skill earns
the surest
      risk,
        the closest to
rolling
     out of control;

             the choice is
not
    in the cabin which barely
lends us shelter,
        the choice is in us
in us:
     what we have heart for,
     to what we are equal:

           the planet
long since gathered torque
         pulsing

the wind this way:
                    as if
we could choose
                    as if
there were choice.

Poem for the Turn of the Century

Wars ago, wars ago
                  this dawn,
the sun come up under cloud,
up and into,
                  men waded ashore
on some June beach
to die.
            At war again
with ourselves
at the century's turn
                  again
we've set sail:
the shore we keep closing on
                  comes clear
through the glass:
on the edge of a village
                  steeped with windmills
people appear
to hill their crop
              with no weapon
beyond a hoe.
In the sinking distance
              we hailed from,
miles aft,
as the sun
           comes over
the cloudbank,

light takes
                    the residual islands
like a wreath
laid on the sea.

When the nurse finally brought in his bedpan,
Noam felt as certain as Luther of wisdom:

Diarrhea spelled backwards, *he told her,*
is, practically, air raid.

Whadidyasay? *she said.* Nothing,
Noam said, I said nothing.

Calendar

Two months after
the birth of her
June child, she found

in her neighbor's
backyard that she
couldn't talk. She

ran inside to
write on a pad
don't worry, and

found she couldn't
write. New Year's night
she'd found a mole

grown wild on her
arm. Too many
lifetimes after

her neighbor held
her, her brother-
in-law came for

the child. She
shouted him out
the backdoor: *Look*

*at me, I'm a
corpse.* . . . He ran.
She came that close.

The dark comes down
in white rooms where it
settles nothing.

The dead go on their own way

Ossipee: November

The dark fold of the land:
steeped hills settling
a pond between them.

Black ice on the pond.
Glacial boulders in brooks
holding snow. Halfway up

the horizon, snowsqualls
tall against sun. A tree points,
spare on the clearcut spine

of a mountain. Wherever
it was the lightplane went down
won't unlock until April.

Ord kept asking:
How'd it happen?
How'd he do it?

Everyone said
nobody knew.

Durward said,
Noam used to say
he'd been some
to a shrink . . .

Jesus, *Ordway*
said, he was
a shrink. You got
to go to one
to be one. It's
like signing-on
with a church.

All's I know,
Durward said,
Noam must've been
some good doctor.
He had himself
a built-in
shit detector.

Finest kind, *Ord said.*
But maybe that's what
clogged him up. Maybe
he couldn't stand
all he knew. Maybe he
didn't have any way
left to feel. A man
sits all day
on the edge of nothing,
after a while he
gets numb and falls in.

Syntax

Short of words in that quick dark
where there was nothing between them,

he longed, in her, for some light verb
which, if she could, would ease him.

Nothing is given.
Nothing is unforgiving.

Still Life

The new-cut key on the blue-paint table.
Your place now. The third-floor door,
the stairwell turn no bed
could get up through. But did.

After you get the boy to sleep
you sit at the blue-paint table.
Tea with nothing. No milk, no honey.

Against the table: the small brass shine.

By the time you lie back down
on the same old mattress
you've decided: strip the blue paint off,
bring the whole thing back to natural.
That's what you promise yourself you'll do.

Do for yourself. For Christmas.

Sorting It Out

At the table she used to sew at,
he uses his brass desk scissors
to cut up his shirt.
                    Not that the shirt
was that far gone: one ragged cuff,
one elbow through;
                    but here he is,
cutting away the collar
she long since turned.
                    What gets to him finally,
using his scissors like a bright claw,
is prying buttons off:
                    after they've leapt,
spinning the floor, he bends
to retrieve both sizes:
                    he intends to
save them in some small box; he knows
he has reason to save; if only he knew
where a small box
                    used to be kept.

Wonder

Wonder what I imagine:
                    that
I imagine.
                    Not as limpets rasp
their mouths to rock, or stalks of kelp
in tide fly blind,
                    imagine how
from them I climbed:
                    to sense
whose eyes my child may have,
to feel at heart the letters
                    cut in time
on my own grave.
                    Imagine:
out of sea, up from algae,
                    bearing
firewood, icons, nightmares,
                    for ages
standing watch or trying to sleep.
No wonder we want sharing:
                    alone
on narrow ledges,
                    being
struck by being,
                    we toss guesses
out before us, dreaming to survive
who so far we've become.

Old Man

This is a dream I needed.

I wake in my own old room
toward morning, lying next to the knees
of a girl—a young mother—born
in the milltown miles upriver.
Kneeling beside me, smiling,
she lets her long hair shelter me from
every view of myself. Except, out the dormer window,
the town's last elm.

I adore you
I tell her.
I know, she says,
with you I am quiet.

This is a sleep I am lucky to wake from.

By the time I walk down over the hill
for the *News*, she is opening her store.
She turns in the doorway, her son in arms,
and smiles. I nod and smile, trusting myself
not to say I adore her, trusting her
to dream what I have not said.

Liv

Not to dream her to bed, not to drink
in mid-age to the shapes of her body an old hand
might cup, nor to sleep in her own dream,

but to wake in some change of one's life
beside her: to measure dayrise in her steeped eye;
first, if ever, now to belong to how her face

assumes morning, and crinkles against
an old anguish into her dearest smile:
now to wake with her: to give prime love

to how her eyes admit of self-possession,
yet yearn, like children strayed to nightmare ice,
for loving and forgiving; forgiven now,

being so enabled by her being: to touch
the day's contingency: to face
with how she looks her ways of seeing.

No matter how I feel,
I am of several minds.

Nothing I think is as sure
as my mind's several voices.

Mary's, After Dinner

Both hands talking, raised to shoulder height,
the left uptilted with a Lucky Strike,
the right still doubled down, inside of smoke,
across an opposite heart:

the argument is nothing,
nothing after all . . .

. . . all August that we've drunk,
made talk of, dined on, drawn back from,
then come back to sip;

the evening settled,
dearly, in your hands, the room
moves to the logic of your smile:
sitting full-face, unsurrender'd,
you say whole strophes from *Anon.,*
the truest poet of all;

more telling
than we knew, their measure
opens us to speak:

before the fire
your calendar has lit, brilliant
for the moment, we let words raise us
by their power:

we hear
our language validate our lives.

Thinking About Hannah Arendt
(1906–1975)

The kitchen stove wood-ash
I took out this morning,
to dress the snowfield
that covers the garden.

The ashwood I've blazed
to fell before dark:
a whole grove to go,
to limb and twitch out,
to yard and fit; then,
after all, let season.

This present fire.
This kitchen oven.

The cigarette smoke you inhaled, held deep,
and let drift, displaced
in Maine, telling
your fear in being a Jew
landing alone in
Damascus. At home
with how slowly
iron heats, with
how strange to
myself I am, I sit
by a stove as dark as
the mourning you wore
against snow. I lean

to the exquisite warmth
of your sadness, your
intricate face:
             your eyes clear
with a reason dear beyond reason.

This Day After Yesterday

Robert Trail Spence Lowell (1917–1977)

I

This day after yesterday.

Morning rain small on the harbor,
nothing that's not gray.

I heard at Hooper's, taking the Plymouth in
for brakes. Out from behind
his rolltop desk, Ken said, "*R*adio says
a *col*league of yours died. Yessir,
*died. Low*ell. Wasn't he your friend?"

Yesterday blazed, the Bay full of spindrift and sun.
If you'd looked down from your Ireland plane
I could have shared you twelve seals upriver,
seven heron in Warm Cove, and
an early evening meteor.

                  If I'd said such portents,
you would have flattened me with prepschool repartee,
your eyes owl'd out:

               "And a poet up a fir tree . . ."

II

That's how friendship went.

At least this summer,

this last summer:
                    home,
almost home.

Ulysses come up over the beachstones,
shuffling with terrible age. We hugged and
parted, up the picnic field,
lugging tens of summers.

III

You wanted women, mail, praise.
What men thought of what you'd conquered.
Beyond the irony of fame, the honor due
to how a poet suffers: the brilliance of first drafts,
the strophe tinker'd into shape, a life
in twelve right lines come almost whole.
You were voluntarily committed: you sweat-out hours
to half-know what the day's poems came to.

Who knows what they did? Or,
by your dying, have?
                    Who knows what word
                    you were bringing home?
                    You, bridging marriages,
                    Ulysses into Queens and through.

An almost final draft
for your collected life,
your unrevisable last poem.

IV

You were a trying man, God knows.
Over drinks, or after, your wit mauled,
twice life sized: like your heroic mattress-chest.

Manic, you were brutal. The brightest boy
in school, the school's most cruel monitor,
you wrenched skin, or twisted arms, as if

Caligula were just. Of those who never made
a team, you were Captain; to them, life-long,
you were Boston-loyal. Guilt in excess

was your subject, not your better nature.
For sheer guts you had no peer. Sane,
you almost seemed God's gentlest creature.

V

Jesus, how death gets to us . . .

On the Common, just this week,

they've jacked up Harriet Winslow's house,
all the front sills gone.

And on the sea-side of the Barn
you wrote in, the bulkhead
finally gave way to the tide.

And then the giving-way you,
like Agee, never got to write:
a poet in a New York cab . . .

VI

Weighed by your dying,
Cal, I find myself

much wanting. How could
I dread you less, or

love you more? Left
time, I try to write

old summers back, as if
you'd never maddened

my perspective. More
in misery than love,

I have your life
by heart. Without you,

I am easier and less:
the planet grays,

the village rot
you left eats through

another step, the Bay
that was our commonplace

is flatter . . .

VII

Everything about me
sags: my body tells

my disbelief its
own mortal story.

I meant to write
a different poem:

> *A seal to tides.*
> *A heron lifted off.*
> *A meteor.*

No. If poems
can be believed,

better how
time conjugates:

> *day by day,*
> *day after day,*
> *this day after yesterday . . .*

a dog with flattened
ears, lying on

old dung, lifts
his muzzle, the lame

best that he can,
to welcome his

old master
home.

> *May all such ghosts attend*
> *your spirit, now. May it,*
> *with them, be lighter.*

Gathering Greens
Donald Dike (*1920–1978*)

In thin snow
blown inland
from sea, all

afternoon I've
tracked into
the woods after

cedar, hemlock,
and spruce. I've
come across

mouse-print,
fox-sign, and
deer run to where

the old dark
spends the night.
I've been here

before, but not
so far in; not
beside partridge

in blow-down, not
to the deeryard
in snow. I need

to learn to
protect myself,
as any animal

must. I try
to learn with
myself to be

gentle: to wait
until light
for the first

shadow to
point me out
to the coast.

Continuum

Tiding the bank
                    all morning
long light streams
in the valley
                    fog scales off
clear upriver
clearing there
                    the bridge
the cables grid
a mountain
                    hemlock
ridged dark
against sky
                    as far as I
can see
my mind's eye bound
                            by the speed
of light
to be partial
                    seeing
who we become
relative to
                    each other's
perspective
exchanging views
                    all

morning long
informed by
                absolute
sun

Lichens

Close to the point a mile upriver
where nuclear waste begins
to waste, close to the end

of the century, the coast weathers
before its next weather: March,
the primary colors still sky,

ocean, granite, spruce, snow;
and in a noon clearing, a knoll
in woods the British once stormed,

the lichens as the sun finds them:
nonflowering pioneer plants,
a low mix of algae and fungi,

they name themselves: Toad Skin
or Map Lichen written on rock,
Reindeer rampant through moss,

British Soldiers in log rot,
and Pale Shield lichen against
the northside of hemlock, rooted

where redcoats fell for nothing,
where man availeth not, where
the wind veers quiet as if March

could prime new life, the lichens
still, the lichens hold,
close to the bone of the planet.

Thoreau Near Home

Seasick off Cape Ann, by moonlight,
on the night boat bound for Portland,
he took a week by mailcoach
tacking inland in hope
of some new school that wanted teaching.
No one listened save an Oldtown Indian.

May 13: looking east from Belfast for
some fairer weather, he booked passage
for Castine, an eight-mile reach, aboard
the sailboat *Cinderilla*.

He found the harbor full: coasters, one
square-rigger, shallops, pulling-boats.
Walking Argyle Street's steep hill, he
step by step rested his whole frame,
that each moment might abide. White clapboard,
spires, and cupolas claimed his eye.
A boy named Philip Hooke pointed to
Fort George, meadowy ramparts crowning
the peninsula. A war ago, boys
hardly men were posted here to die.

No, no teaching offered here.
By another spring, he thought, I
may be a Greenland whaler or
mail-carrier in Peru. All answers
being in the future, day answering

to day, he studied, into evening, how
merchants and how seamen paced their lives.
Bright as roadside shadblow
the night came fresh with stars.
He stayed the night at Deborah Orr's.

Captain Skinner, on the morning packet
back to Belfast, kept the poems of Burns
shelved in his cabin. As strewn clouds cleared,
Thoreau took the deck and looked back at the cliffs
that had not heard of Emerson.
The village shone.

Within a week, Thoreau would be home;
two months from now he would be twenty-one.
He stood watch on Castine, the farthest east
he ever sailed. He thought back to the *Iliad* and Homer;
he found the day fit for eternity, and saw
how sunlight fell on Asia Minor.

All night the wind
says what it says.
Blind to the moment,
I lie back into
the depth of my life,
pretending to know
the trees' translation.

The Valley Road

Before eight,
the sun already hours up
into May, the thin
children come out.

Clustered
in front of shut
housetrailer doors,
or farmsteads gone to
dry rot,
                    they open
like laughter:
                              loose-
strife, bluet, star-
flower, arbutus,
                              early
at every
schoolbus stop.

Tree Nursery

Infinite rows of calm,
hundreds of sizes of stretch.

Plot upon plot, they give
themselves to the sun to true up.

They ladder the eye.
Colors from spruce to beech,

lilac trying to spring,
maple left gold from fall.

Every one planted to cross
the horizon. Antennae,

arms, hourglasses, arches,
roots inverted to victories:

not one branch in infinity
fails to take its own shape.

By self-definition
I cannot measure
a particle of myself,
not even the wavelength
of my own shadow. How
can I shape what I feel?
Beyond naming names,
nothing can help.
I learn my limits,
I write what I can;
I didn't become
a poet for nothing.

Tools

To get a handle on how
the day may work: a wedge

to split chunks off, a bar
with good purchase

to bring them home; saws,
next, to rip out grain,

then crosscut what lengths
come to: the grandfather head

of one man's hammer;
the day's ash hung

by spokeshave and rasp
to fit the arc

it strikes
against morning's turning:

by evening maybe
something to

show for: words
that name what shape

day took, or
one may still imagine.

Eaton's Boatyard

To make do, making a living:
                              to throw away nothing,
practically nothing, nothing that may
come in handy:
                        within an inertia of caked paintcans,
frozen C-clamps, blown strips of tarp, and
pulling-boat molds,
                    to be able to find,
for whatever it's worth,
                            what has to be there:
the requisite tool
                        in this culch there's no end to:
the drawshave buried in potwarp,
chain, and manila jibsheets,
                                or, under the bench,
the piece that already may fit
                              the idea it begins
to shape up:
                    not to be put off by split rudders,
stripped outboards, half
a gasket, and nailsick garboards:
                                to forget for good
all the old year's losses,
                        save for
what needs be retrieved:
                            a life given to

how today feels:
                    to make of what's here
what has to be made
to make do.

Nothing is more than
simple absence: no father,
no tree to lean on,
no current to ride,
no rock off the shore
to feel a toe down to.

Nothing, at bottom,
is to have nothing
at heart: no self left
who will hear one's
other self speak, no
sense that relates
to another sense,
feeling nothing
permeate everything.

Nothing has meaning.
Nothing means what
it says: the acute
presence of absence:
the who I am not,
the where God isn't,
the void the dead leave,
the when I am dead.

Nothing is infinite absence
invading the finite truth

of my life: my own absence
from years of mornings,
the emptying-out of self
I cannot avoid, the void
of not being I cannot
learn to believe in.

Building Her

Wood: learning it:
                        feeling the tree
shiver the helve, feeling the grain
resist the saw, feeling for grain
with adze and chisel, feeling the plank
refuse a plane, the voyage of sap
still live in the fiber;
                        joining wood:
scarfing it, rabbeting keel and sternpost,
matching a bevel, butting a joint
or driving a trunnel:
                        whatever fastens
the grain, the grain lets in, and binds;

let wood breathe or keep wood briny,
wood will outlive generations:

working wood, a man learns how
wood works:
                        wood comes and goes
with weather or waves; wood gives:

come to find right grain for timbers,
keelson, stem, a man can feel
how wood remembers:
                                the hull will
take to sea the way the tree knew wind.

Nothing answers to
nothing. Nothing
else. The question
is not how to outlive
life, but how
—in the time we're
possessed by—to face
the raw beauty of being.

Dayrise

At first light I hear miles of silence.
Except for the First Selectman's snowtires
snuffling up Main Street, it's Sunday-quiet;

half awake, knowing that deer season's done,
I dream of does wounded, bedded in spruce groves.
And bucks downed in the bog, who had last night

to give up. I doze with Han-Shan, the old T'ang drunk,
who took to Cold Mountain after the capital
turned down his poems. The woodfire's dying;

I get myself up to stoke it, rewrite night-notes
next to the stove, and wake my wife. After breakfast,
before I try to home-in on today's unwritten poem,

we go out into winter to fell next year's wood:
with her small ax and my stuttering saw, we cut near the bog,
on the low spruce crown of the woodlot we call Cold Knoll.

Given this day, none
better, I stretch to
let trees revive me;
I allow the dead
recall themselves;
I behold nothing,
forgive God; I tell
myself to change
be native: I bare
myself, sleep moved
by stars, take dreams
toward morning; I want
with trees to affect
the day: to lend joy,
accept pain, give
without question;
as trees, beyond doubt,
face prevailing light,
I let love wake me:
I extend myself to
every reflection, as
I have to, to feel for
the planet: nowhere
better, with nothing
to lose, than here
to give thanks
life takes place.

Soundings

Change   that cannot
be changed.   Who
we were: who knows
what was true?   Or is.
We used to dream islands.
Now we think woodlots.

You haven't touched the piano
for years, for years I believed
you'd give my words music.

Change   the old constant
change: where morning sun was,
how fog comes in over Cape Rosier:
for years and years over and over
in streams, wisps, bankings, whole clouds
at a time.   This afternoon again
it was different.   You, going gray,
have grown new, you've touched me
to lean to see how you feel.

Changing   what moves us
changes: we move with fog
into new coves and settle ourselves
in peninsular woods.   As I go
to fell oak I can hear your hands
gaining their way back up the piano.

Before Sleep

The day put away before bed,
the house almost closed before night.

By the time I walk out over the knoll,
down the steep Main Street

that dead-ends in the sea,
the village has put out its lights.

The winter stars are turned up over
the tide, a tide so quiet the harbor

holds stars. The planet holds.
Before the village turns over in sleep,

I stand at the edge of the tide,
letting my feet feel into the hillside

to where my dead ancestors live.
Whatever I know before sleep

surrounds me. I cannot help know.
By blood or illness, gossip or hope,

I'm relative to every last house.
Before I climb home up the hill, I hold:

I wait for myself to quiet, breathing
the breath of sleepers I cannot help love.

The House in the Trees

Within an island of trees in the space of nature
it is barely there.
                        Hard to discover,
strange to remember the way.
                                The house in the trees
is constantly being arrived at.
It conforms to the hillside, it receives light
as a guest. There is no wind in the trees,
but the house trembles
                        on the verge of being lived in.
It wants paint
                to define its existence, it takes on color
containing the air around it. Walls emerge
in every advent of weather,
                            a house in the process
of being built, of building:
Cézanne said
            I am its consciousness.
Waiting it out, he watched himself making it happen:
within an island of trees, a human
plenitude at the center. This is the house
every day he painted
                        he took to sleep and woke up in,
barely clothed in the freedom of knowing
before it could ever be done
he would have, finally, to leave it.

CAMERA NORTH

PHILIP BOOTH teaches in the Creative
Writing Program at Syracuse University each
spring but spends as much of the year as
possible at his home in Maine. This is his
sixth book. The latest in a long line of honors
bestowed upon him is a 1980 Fellowship in
Writing from the National Endowment for
the Arts. Most of the poems in *Before Sleep*
were composed in the hundred-and-thirty-
year-old family house where the author's
grandparents lived, and where his grandson
represents the fifth generation.